WHAT PEOPLE A
THE ICE CREAM

The Ice Cream Vendor's Son, recent collection of mystical flash fiction, seduces with a voice more compelling than the mythical siren's call. But this is an enticement that you don't want to resist. Holland's superbly imaginative prose probes a deeper understanding of the human condition and touches tender, guarded places in our hearts. Her memorable characters explore hidden layers of existence, some beyond the grave or across parallel planes. Each of the forty-six stories delivers a uniquely flavored life lesson about love, grief, loss, hope, revenge, dreams or illusions. You'll want to savor them all in one reading and then return again and again for another taste.

– *Nancy Pogue LaTurner, author of* Voluntary Nomads

I know there is not such a thing as "surrealistic realism," although Laura McHale Holland's book of flash fiction did elicit that term from me as I devoured her characters, unsettling but yet inspiring. Trees grow from empty boxes, a woman receives a passionate kiss from a stranger in the middle of a horrific accident, a girl has a love affair with a snake, there is an imagined blackened sky of birds, dancing shoes, a wild girl and lots of just plain folks in images of love, hate and wonderment, and it goes on, until the last story when a soft whisper of "wow" escaped my lips.

Holland is an innovative story teller of the lives of normal people, your neighbors and friends who are not in the least bit normal. I pondered often in the reading, how close are we to what folks want to happen but only dare imagine or wish. This is a book for writers who want to see the craft at its best and for readers who want to be titillated and thoroughly amazed. I know I was.

– *Linda Loveland Reid, author of* Touch of Magenta

I'm one of Laura McHale Holland's big fans. Her stories are edgy, chilling, laugh-out-loud, make you cry and always emotionally charged. I've had the pleasure of reading her entire collection, and ... all I can say is keep 'em coming.
  – Ana Manwaring, author of Zihuatanejo

Laura Mchale Holland, author of Reversible Skirt, *writes with musicality and a unique, dream-like quality. With elements ranging from realist to surrealist, often within the same piece, the selection of flash fiction in* The Ice Cream Vendor's Song *will surprise readers and leave them wanting more.*

Here are ordinary men and women as well as those who are insane, children, animals and ghosts–all taking part in this diurnal and nocturnal theater of the wonderful, dark and absurd. Diverse in subject, form and nature, these condensed stories are worth reading and rereading, so that one might savor the many layers of meaning, mystery and relatable humanity.
  – Yu-Han Chao – author of We Grow Old

Laura McHale Holland's stories are elegant, eerily haunting and often beautiful.
  – Sunny Lockwood, author of Shades of Love

Modern fables with ... layers of meaning hidden in metaphor, revealed in raw emotion and haunting in their sudden intimacy.
  – Kate Farrell, editor of the Wisdom Has a Voice *anthology*

The Ice Cream Vendor's Song

The Ice Cream Vendor's Song

FLASH FICTION

Laura McHale Holland

WORDFOREST
Rohnert Park, California

The Ice Cream Vendor's Song
© 2012 Laura McHale Holland

All rights reserved. No part of this book may be used or reproduced in any manner—except for brief quotations in literary articles or reviews—without written permission of the author. For information contact the publisher, Wordforest, Rohnert Park, California; http://wordforest.com; mailing address P.O. Box 7501, Cotati, CA 94931.

The characters and events portrayed in this book are fictitious. Any similarity to real persons, living or dead, is purely coincidental.

ISBN: 978-0-9829365-3-5

Library of Congress Control Number: 2012943670

Cover and book design by Kathy McHale, www.mchalecreative.com
Author photo by Jason Figueroa, www.photography-by-jason.com

Early drafts of the stories in this collection were posted on http://lauramchaleholland.com.

For the kind readers who have followed my blog–week in, week out. You are the reason this book came to be.

Contents

They Knew Not	... 1
Still There	... 3
She Could Decide	... 4
Rolling Toward Her Feet	... 6
The Kiss	... 7
Her Love Returns	... 8
The Fool	... 10
The Wild One	... 11
It's Just a Job	... 13
Creep Him Out	... 15
The Golden Sandals	... 16
He Never Asked	... 19
The Hunted	... 20
The Endless Night	... 21
One of These Days	... 23
My Tormentors	... 25
The Neighborly Thing	... 26
Long Gone	... 29
Drawn In	... 31
Counting	... 35
Something Ordinary	... 36
Feral Cats	... 37
Four Blocks Away	... 39

I'll Have to Tell Him	... 40
What For	... 43
Life Along the Coast	... 45
The Wrong Man	... 46
Never, Ever	... 47
Disappointed	... 49
How Dreadful	... 50
A Dove Coos	... 51
I Don't Suppose	... 52
Better Things to Do	... 53
She'll Be Ready	... 54
Squished a Spider	... 55
She Couldn't Wait	... 56
Drifting	... 57
My First Love	... 58
Snow Colors	... 59
Since the Accident	... 61
Tears Will Slow	... 62
Thanks, I Guess	... 63
When She Wakes Up	... 65
Music for Ghosts	... 67
Tide Pool Dream	... 68
The Ice Cream Vendor's Song	... 69

They Knew Not

Keys in hand, she shuffled up the drive. She'd had a long day cashiering at a nearby convenience store and was picturing the wilting veggies in the fridge she'd have to use right away or toss. She didn't notice the package by the front door until her sneaker bumped it.

About the size of a shoebox, the parcel was wrapped in brown paper. Her name and address were printed in bold black letters. No return address. Once inside, she unwrapped the package. It was just an empty cardboard box.

She tried to squish the box so it wouldn't take up too much room in her recycling bin, but it was surprisingly sturdy. It wouldn't even smash when she jumped up and down on it, nor could she cut it with scissors or a box cutter. So she threw it whole into the bin. It was carted away a few days later.

The next week, she arrived home and found a package wrapped in brown paper. It was the same, empty box, or one exactly like it. She buried it that night in the middle of her backyard.

The next morning a sapling stood where she'd buried the box. Over the next several months it grew into a sturdy tree that flowered and bore an exotic fruit: blue pears. She thought the pears might be poisonous, but she couldn't resist tasting one. It was delicious, sweet, juicy, intoxicating.

She took a wheel barrow of the pears to the local farmers market, where word of their delectable taste spread quickly. Every week thereafter the tree produced more exquisite, azure pears. And every week she went to the market and sold them all.

People couldn't get enough of them. Children cried for the taste of their juice; judges on the bench fantasized about biting into their cerulean flesh; restaurants clamored for them; artists drew murals of sparkling blue pears in the town square. The local newspaper wrote a feature article about her pears. She said the tree had grown in her yard on its own. She didn't mention the box. Who would have believed her anyway?

She quit her job and developed a booming cottage industry. She made all manner of products from her prized pears: pies, cobblers, jams, jellies, soaps, lotions, balms, perfumes, incense, even blue pear charms and other trinkets. She and the town prospered for decades until one day, old, gray and feeble, she took to her bed.

She left her home, business and considerable savings to her nephew and his wife. But the precious pear tree died the day they moved in. A couple months later, an empty box appeared at their door. They were having guests over for a barbeque that night to celebrate a state-of-the-art outdoor kitchen they'd put in right where the pear tree used to flower. They used the box as kindling for their fire pit. The flames were deep blue and mesmerizing.

Nothing grew from the ashes; no more empty boxes appeared at their door. But they didn't suffer, for they knew not what they'd burned.

Still There

He told her he was done. No more. The shrill voice, the cantaloupes rotting on the counter, rows of yellowed newspapers stacked to the ceiling, the ivy encroaching, blocking out the sun. The years filled with promises broken. He'd had enough.

She sat in her recliner as usual. The TV blared another episode of *The Real Housewives of New Jersey*. Southern Comfort bottles rattled on the floor as trucks zoomed along the nearby freeway.

"I'm not coming back, Mom," he said. "Not until you do something for yourself, make some kind of effort." Her skeletal tabby meowed and rubbed against his legs. "I'm taking Daisy with me," he said. "You don't even care about her anymore."

He lifted the cat in his arms and stomped out the door, slamming it closed with his foot. The home creaked. A condolence card fell from the mantle and landed in her lap.

The card was still there two weeks later when her landlord stopped in. Newspapers had piled up on her front porch, and she wasn't answering the phone.

The coroner estimated she'd been dead at least a month.

She Could Decide

Aggie white-knuckles the steering wheel as she speeds the old Volvo down Mountain Highway. New clicks coming from the engine poke a million tiny cracks in the morning calm. She wants to scream.

She slows as she approaches a familiar intersection, brakes to a stop, rests her head on the steering wheel. Half an hour or more could pass before she sees another car pass by.

It's been three days since she's slept. Three days since she's been home. Three weeks since she's gone to work. Three weeks since Bill went in for what the doctor said was routine surgery. Three weeks since he failed to wake up.

Home is to the right, just a few miles down the hill. Home, newspapers yellowing in the driveway, Bill's fishing pole by the door. Home, a shower, a change of clothes. Home, food spoiling in the fridge, a red light flashing for voicemail waiting. Home is to the right.

In the passenger seat, Aggie sees the tartan scarf Bill left behind, the information about the Grand Canyon she'd downloaded and printed out to bring to the hospital. They were going to go as soon as Bill recovered, maybe even ride the mules down to the bottom. She sees the case of CDs Bill burned before he got an iPhone. She unzips it, puts a CD into the player and turns the car to the left.

Familiar guitar licks fill the car. It's the Ventures' *Walk Don't Run*. The electric chords vibrate to her bones. She becomes a human mandolin, a drum set, a jazz dancer, an airplane soaring to the sky as the car chugs up the hill. She turns the music up as far as it will go, pulls the car over near a trail she and Bill have walked many times. She gets out of the car, dances around it and then gyrates along the trail, redwoods swaying overhead.

The trail leads to a footbridge over a winding creek. A bridge she loves. A creek Bill loves. She sees Bill twirling toward the bridge from the other side. They meet in the center of the bridge, and when their fingertips touch they are both jitterbugging, twisting and hitch hiking in their junior high school gym. They dance on and on until Aggie drops, exhausted and old to the wooden planks of the bridge.

Bill keeps on dancing. He is old, too, but dancing as though he'd just begun. He dances backward into the forest. He looks content, matter of fact.

Aggie sits up, wraps her arms around her legs, puts her forehead against her knees and cries for the first time since the doctor insisted only she could decide whether to pull the plug.

Rolling Toward Her Feet

She is vertical on the veranda; he is horizontal in the grass. She weaves her love for him in shades of blue, green and purple his colorblind eyes cannot see. He sands his love for her on boards of oak and pine that give her splinters. Her songs of love catch in the wind and fly like lost kites far from his grasp while his poems turn to quicksand on her dresser.

They have schedules, cable bills, best friends from far away. They have children unborn, waiting in their rosebush hedge, in the woodpile, in their gravy boat gathering dust in the corner. His skin is raw from hauling cinderblock anger night and day; her fingers are burned by fear boiling in her oatmeal.

She is on the veranda, leaning forward. He is in the grass, rolling toward her feet.

The Kiss

She worried as she walked the buckled pavement past broken storefront windows, dangling fire escapes and leaning Victorians. But it wasn't the safety of her husband and children, nor the condition of her home that concerned her. The crew that pried the doors off the streetcar holding her and a slew of screaming passengers said the quake's epicenter was 100 miles away; local damage had been minimal, all things considered.

She worried, but not about the work she'd lose before everything returned to normal, and not about the gash on her arm and bump on her head.

She worried about the kiss. The kiss from a stranger who drew her close as the streetcar erupted in turmoil. When the car shook and shrieked and sputtered, the man who had been quietly texting in the seat beside her gave her a Rhett Butler kiss. And when she thought she was losing everything in the world she holds dear, she kissed him back. She kissed him back with all the fire of Scarlet O'Hara, a fire she'd never before known.

As the rumbling died down and the streetcar stopped rocking, as she and the stranger disentangled and averted their eyes, as she took a rescue worker's hand and stepped onto blessed solid ground, she worried that whether or not she told her husband about the kiss, it would plague her marriage like bacteria eating through tender flesh.

Her Love Returns

She fell in love with a python when she was fifteen. She met him in her backyard. She saw a flash of gold near the hot tub gazebo and gave chase, cornering it in the bamboo that had taken over a swath of earth by the fence. Their eyes locked in the moment. Hers were darkest brown; the serpent's were an emerald green, glowing against his body of golden scales. He shimmered even in the shade.

There was no need to talk. They shared each other's thoughts, enraptured. They began meeting in the bamboo each day after school. She stroked his long torso with slender hands; he twined around her body and pressed a little harder each day.

One afternoon her mother came out with some vegetable scraps to add to the compost bin and saw a glint of gold in the bamboo. Uncertain what she might find, she grabbed an axe leaning against the fence near the bin and tiptoed over to the bamboo. There she saw her daughter limp in the snake's grasp. The mother whacked at the serpent once, twice, thrice. Golden liquid seeped from the wounds and pooled in the dirt. The snake unwound and slithered away.

The mother carried her unconscious daughter to the car and sped to the hospital. When she awoke three days later, the girl asked about the python. Gone, she was told, and thank goodness. When she was released from the hospital, the first thing she did was run to the bamboo, but there was no sign of the python. In the dirt, though, was the gold that had trickled from the snake's wounds, now solid and shaped into a ball that fit perfectly into her palm.

That was two years ago. The family doctor says the girl suffered brain damage from lack of oxygen. The mother agrees with the doctor because the girl takes such a long time to answer even the simplest questions like, What day is it? or Where do you live? The girl knows better, though, for every morning before school she sits up in bed and holds the golden ball. She closes her eyes, and her love returns to her. They entwine in bliss until her mother calls to her and says it's time for breakfast. She's told no one about her morning trysts. She'd rather they think she's brain damaged than crazy.

The Fool

Teeth clenched, she slashes her machete through a row of silk blouses and slinky sheaths, then crouches in the closet as laughter bubbles up from a foyer that used to be hers. He'd filed for divorce one month into her three-year term, a sentence she'd earned for embezzling to pay his gambling debts. Since then, he'd changed his phone number, his hair style, his bank, his job, his wife—but he hadn't changed the lock on the front door. The fool.

The Wild One

Old Pete left the ranch to his three grown kids. The two sons were too busy helping their offspring with algebra, fixing leaking roofs, launching Internet startups and such to take over the place. They wanted to sell, and I was set to buy. Until his daughter, the Wild One, put her foot down, said she wanted to move back home, run the place herself.

I'll say this for her, she's belligerent. She wore her brothers down.

She left her barista job and second-hand lover in some West Coast hamlet and moved back here to Wyoming, her Subaru wagon filled with ripped jeans, patchwork jackets, tarot cards, marijuana and non-diet, diet books like *Skinny Bitch* and *Women, Food and God*.

Almost as soon as the she slipped her tattooed body through the front door it was one long party at Old Pete's place. As far as I can tell she didn't mend one fence or even saddle up a horse. She was too busy painting her toenails and posting hourly updates on Twitter. Meanwhile, all the animals were starving. I couldn't stand it, especially seeing Pete's dog, Spike, turn to skin and bones.

I complained to her brothers, but like I said, they were busy. They didn't want any headaches, and they didn't believe me anyway.

So I stole Spike, and then some of the horses. The Wild One didn't notice. If I'd stopped my thieving then, the remaining horses would have died, and the cattle, too. So I crept into Old Pete's house late one night and shocked her senseless with a taser gun I bought online. Then I carried her home and locked her in a soundproof basement room where I used to have a recording studio.

When I bring the Wild One oatmeal each morning she asks when I'm going to set her free, but I don't answer. She'll never wear me down. You see, I stole her freedom. I stole it and I'm glad I did.

Everyone thinks she ran off with a new lover, so Old Pete's place is up for sale again, and I'm set to buy it. I think Pete would be okay with this because Spike is fat and happy, sleeping at my feet. And his wayward daughter has settled down at last.

It's Just a Job

Dwane holds her ring in the palm of his hand and stares at six small diamonds circling a larger one. They all reflect the sunlight breaking through the slit where the curtains never quite close. The ring is traditional, just like her. "It's beautiful, Margaret," he says.

She smiles, toothless, and nods as he dabs his fingertips on the smooth gold band. He stares at the treasure. It would be so easy to enclose it in his fist, slip it into his pocket and leave. As though reading his mind, she tugs on the white cuff of his jacket, takes his palm in her hands and presses it closed around the ring. She nods again and puts her index finger to her lips with a shhh.

"No, dear. I can't," Dwane says, wishing Margaret's last stroke hadn't silenced her. He had enjoyed her so, and she'd seemed to genuinely care about him. She'd remembered that his wife loves white roses, that little Betts hates onions, that Jeff is the goalie for his soccer team—all the little details that show someone is paying attention.

He sits on the edge of Margaret's bed, takes her left hand in his, as her groom once did, and tries to slip the ring back on the slender finger that wore it for more than half a century. She yanks her hand away, curls into a ball on the bed and starts to rock. He stands up, straightens his uniform and drops the ring in his pocket.

"I'll see you later," he says. "Maybe I'll pick you up for Bingo after lunch. Would you like that, Margaret?"

| IT'S JUST A JOB

She rocks harder. He lifts her breakfast tray from where she'd left it, untouched, on the stand by her bed, places it on his cart, turns and leaves the room.

At the end of the hall, he stops in at the nurses' station, hands the nurse on duty the ring. She puts it in a safe and says, "Yeah, poor Margaret. She's losing her marbles fast. Her family will appreciate this."

"I suppose they will," Dwane replies.

Driving home after a long shift, he can't stop tears from filling his eyes. He's supposed to keep his distance, not get attached; it's just a job. He's helping people let go with dignity. That's it. He pulls into his driveway and parks. He stays at the wheel for just a minute. The shadows of his wife and children dance on the picture window drapes as he readies to go inside and wrap each one of them in his arms.

Creep Him Out

Their caw, caw, cawing pelts Wendy's ears like gunshot. She stumbles as she dashes, hands over her ears, from front porch to carport. Why the murder of crows gathers so often in the pines shading her townhouse she doesn't know.

Their blue-black bodies darken the trees; their yellow eyes follow her as she settles into her Mazda and fastens the seatbelt. She starts the engine and backs out of the drive. Their cacophony penetrates her refuge. They swarm from tree to tree in her wake as she speeds down familiar streets on her way to work. She turns up the volume on her CD player, hoping Freddy Mercury's voice soaring on *Bohemian Rhapsody* will embolden her. But the caws intensify, and the music grows fainter each time she turns up the volume.

By the time Wendy reaches the office, her heart is pounding, her breath is coming in short bursts and she is sweating through her clothes. Hundreds of crows alight in the pine trees edging the parking lot. She turns off the engine but can't bring herself to open the door. She sits. The crows quiet down. She knows they'll go away if she waits long enough.

Inside, Wendy's boss looks out his window. He sees no crows, only Wendy, still as a mannequin in her car. Why she stares, without blinking, up at the trees instead of coming into the office he doesn't know. It seems to happen every couple of weeks. And when she finally comes inside a sour smell permeates the office. It's starting to creep him out.

The Golden Sandals

Carole saw the ad on Facebook. The sandals. Golden. Shimmering. Three-inch heels. On the right-hand side when she'd clicked on Susan's page. She'd gone there to see pictures of their recent vacation in Costa Rica. Oh, the kisses from strangers. Oh, the tropical breezes. On their last night there, they'd danced the night away at a little club right on the beach.

Carole meant just to look at the pictures and leave a comment; she hadn't even unpacked yet. But she couldn't take her eyes off those sandals. She recalled that last night of vacation. How she'd wished she could dance on and on and never go home to her job as a pharmacy clerk in Oakland. She didn't need new shoes, especially not sandals. She already had thirty pair. But these were so elegant with straps that tied just over the ankle bone. They'd be great dancing shoes, she surmised. And that shimmer mesmerized her.

She clicked on the ad and arrived at a website that offered just about every pair of designer shoes Carole had ever longed for. And she couldn't believe the discount on the sandals. They were by the up-and-coming designer Diablo. If she bought a pair that night, the ad said, she'd be one of the very first women to own a pair. The retail price was $500; they were on sale for $99.99, shipping included, no tax. She was at the checkout page in a matter of seconds, filling in credit card info she'd provided so often on other sites that she had every detail memorized, including that three-number code on the back of her Visa card. She was so excited she could hardly sleep that night.

Four days later, she came home from work and found the shoes by her front door. She knew it was her sandals; the box was the right size. She didn't give any thought to the lack of a return address. She had only a few minutes to get ready to go out. She and several friends were going to a local club where their friend, a DJ, would be working, so they were going to get in for free. She put on a form-fitting black skirt and blouse and gold accessories. Then she slipped on the shoes and began dancing right there in front of her bedroom mirror. Just a little at first.

When she heard Susan's car pull up outside, she danced out to the car. She'd never felt so graceful, so coordinated as she maneuvered herself into the crowded back seat. All the way to the club, she couldn't sit still. Her friends thought she must be high. "What are you on?" they asked. "I'm just excited. You're a bunch of party poopers," she replied. "Could you at least sit still until we get there?" Susan asked. Carole didn't even attempt to stop shuffling and bopping in the car. She was having too much fun.

At the club, she raced to the head of the line and begged, while dancing, for the guy at the door to let her in. He waved her in. She pointed to her friends, who were at the end of the line. He waved them in, too. Carole danced ahead. Soon she was in the center

| THE GOLDEN SANDALS

of the dance floor, stepping and dipping with whoever was willing. But one after another her dance partners tired and had to sit down. Soon all eyes were on the young woman in the sparkling golden sandals who stomped and twirled and spun around and around, whether a song was playing or not. She danced on and on. Her head and shoulders began to droop, her eyes became dull, she heaved and gasped, her black outfit, wet with sweat, clung to her skin. But her feet wouldn't stop. She tried to sit down many times, but her feet kept moving. She tried to take the sandals off, but she couldn't untie the straps. And it seemed, as time went on, her feet propelled her with increasing force.

She called to her friends, begged them to hold her down. They all tried to grasp her, tried to hold her still, but their hands kept slipping right off. She danced on and on. All anyone could do was watch. And when the club closed, she danced out the door with her friends chasing behind. But instead of going to Susan's car, she danced down the street. Her friends ran after her but could not keep up. They collapsed on the sidewalk and watched her dance off into the distance. Twirling, spinning, too winded to even cry out for help. She disappeared on the horizon, and nobody ever saw her again. Not in Oakland anyway.

He Never Asked

The old man eats Cocoa Krispies from a plastic bowl high up in the branches of an elm tree that doesn't exist anymore. But he's there anyway, in a place between life and death. He savors the flavors melding in his mouth as he takes in the sights, smells and sounds of long ago. He watches his childhood friends, girls in ponytails and pigtails, boys in crew cuts, all wearing faded shorts and sporting scabbed knees and elbows as they rollerskate down the block.

The old man's former self is among them, 10 years old, eyeing Susie, the girl who'd just moved in next door. He'd hoped the new neighbors would have a boy his age, not a girl.

The man places his empty cereal bowl and spoon on a nearby branch, but they sail up and away into the clouds, a reminder he is joining a world with different rules. Station wagons come and go below. Mothers in shirtwaist dresses unload and stash groceries and dish out snacks to barefoot children breezing in and out of screen doors. The afternoon wears on.

Children splash in a creek near the house. The old man watches his young self sitting on the grassy bank, his skin drying in the warm wind as Susie approaches, sits down next to him and offers him a charm. It's a pink collie from a box of Cracker Jacks. "Thanks," he says as he lifts it from her moist palm. The boy wonders how she knew *Lassie* was his favorite TV show.

The old man doesn't know the answer; in all the years he and Susie were married, he never asked.

The Hunted

They held hands as they strolled along Main Street. He wore a tuxedo he'd picked up for two bucks at the Salvation Army. She wore a red leotard, red cape and red shoes pulled from the free box at the community center.

The shopkeepers, the moms with toddlers in tow, the office workers sipping their morning Joe all averted their eyes and gave the couple a wide berth. For his feet were bare and hairy, and his head shone with silver wolf's fur. His fangs gleamed in the sunlight when he smiled at his companion, whose face was obscured by the crimson cape's hood.

The two reached the end of Main and turned left onto a path that led to the woods, as a man in mud-splattered jeans, rumpled flannel shirt and baseball cap wobbled out of a corner bar. Seeing the wolf and girl walking into the woods, he stumbled to his truck, grabbed a shotgun and trundled off in pursuit.

Five days later, his body was found floating in the river that rippled through the woods. The word on the street was that the town drunk must have lost his footing, slipped into the water and hit his head on a boulder near the bank.

Meanwhile, the couple who had strolled down Main Street sat in their cabin deep in the woods. They looked like an ordinary man and woman long accustomed to each other's company as they played gin rummy and stole admiring glances at the shotgun mounted above their front door.

The Endless Night

Out of the toxic sludge, the swirl of limp parrots and cut glass, ripped maps and broken bricks, oil spurting and trees uprooted and car parts spinning, out of this, rose a man in silver: cap, trench coat, gloves, pants and boots dripping dead fish and turpentine. He came up from the muck one sodden step at a time, his serpentine tongue darting at flames flickering on boats upended as he chewed Mentos with his pointed teeth.

A blue-skinned family eyed him as they huddled against the only wall remaining on what was once a quaint seashore lane. A father, daughter and son in shredded clothes that hung in strips from their gaunt frames sat on wet concrete slabs and held their hands over a hissing fire. The mother rocked on a milk crate nearby and cooed to a dead baby wrapped in a bloodstained chunk of berber carpet. She did not look up as the man approached.

The man stopped at the fire, clasped his hands and stretched them out to crack his knuckles, but each crack was a lion's roar, deafening the family. They covered their ears, except for the mother. She started singing *All Through the Night*. From behind the wall, faint harpsichord harmony arose.

"It's time," the silver man said. "No!" the father cried. He stood up, raised his arms, lunged forward. The man pulled a pistol from his pocket and fired. From the barrel blasted thousands of radioactive gnats that enveloped the father in a writhing fog so thick he could not breathe. He fell, coughing, to the concrete.

| THE ENDLESS NIGHT

The silver man put the pistol back in his pocket and motioned, palms up, fingers curled, for the children to come to him. They obeyed. When they reached him, he turned and put one arm around each child. Together, the three walked into the sludge and slowly sank into the muck. The harpsichord stopped; the mother kept singing all through the endless night.

One of These Days

Katy slows her pace, despite the biting cold. Carly and Miranda are half a block ahead. She wishes she'd waited a little longer to leave school, so they wouldn't catch her coveting their confidence. The last thing she wants is to be only a few steps behind the queen bees of seventh grade so they can turn, sneer and say something snide like they always do, that is, if they even notice her at all.

Miranda and Carly stop at the corner, their silky light brown hair flowing down their backs. Katy wonders why they've come to a halt, especially since the thermometer has dropped 10 degrees in the last half hour. They're supposed to turn right and walk to the old part of town where the trees are tall and the homes spacious. Then Katy can turn to the left and disappear into her neighborhood of tract homes slapped together a few decades ago, two floor plans alternating block after block.

Katy thinks of crossing the street but dismisses that idea. She has no reason to cross to the right since her home is toward the left. So she plods, hoping Miranda and Carly will have turned right before she reaches the corner. No such luck. They swivel around when Katy draws close.

"Gee, Katy, where ya goin'?" Carly taunts.

"Home," Katy says, head down.

Miranda shoves Katy backward. "You don't have a home, freak. You've got a hovel."

Carly rushes behind to rip Katy's backpack off.

Miranda keeps shoving, throwing Katy off balance.

"Whee, lookee," Carly says as she unzips the backpack and throws Katy's papers and books into the air. The books sink into the snow in a nearby yard; the papers scatter in the wind. Then Carly throws the empty backpack down and joins Miranda in shoving Katy down onto the sidewalk.

Miranda and Carly run off, laughing. "Don't ever follow us again, stalker," Carly calls back to Katy, who is pulling herself up. "Yeah, stay out of our way," Miranda says.

Katy brushes off her coat, picks up her belongings, trudges home. She unlocks the door, sets her wet books and papers out on the table to dry and walks into her mother's bedroom. At the dresser, she opens the second drawer, moves aside some underwear and picks up a handgun. It's not loaded. She hasn't yet figured out where her mom hides the bullets.

She caresses the gun barrel, rubs it against her cheek. "One of these day, old gun. One of these days we'll get even," she whispers. Then she tucks the gun back beneath the underwear, skips into the kitchen and pours herself a glass of chocolate milk.

My Tormentors

They lurk in the spaces between words, in the pause before the stoplight changes from yellow to red. Always the same burgundy hue, they shift shapes, stand on the roof, slip into the junk drawer, crawl across palm fronds lining the sidewalk. Knowing if they can nick me, I will be theirs, infected.

They fly overhead now, pterodactylesque, their huge wings beating in counterpoint to my breath. I run, run, but then I stumble. After a lifetime of eluding them, I falter, wonder why I bother to resist. They sweep down; scratch my shoulders, arms, face; and then fly off.

I hurry home, shower, put Neosporin on my wounds. But as I dress, my toes turn into claws, my arms become wings. My eyes shrink; my tongue darts out, my heart, still warm, pounds. Up, up, I go now chasing to the clouds my tormentors.

The Neighborly Thing

It started on a Wednesday in March, about 1:30 in the afternoon. Mary Buehl heard it first, the country music blaring from Fred and Lula Hentzel's garage on Maple Street. Fred loved country music. And since he'd retired back in January, he'd been tinkering in his garage most afternoons, crooning along to the likes of Merle Haggard, Patsy Cline, Garth Brooks, Keith Urban, Carrie Underwood. But the volume reached a new level that afternoon, one Mary found intolerable.

Then Brady Freeman heard it. He was walking his retriever around the block like he always did at that time of day, and he noticed it as soon as he rounded the corner onto Maple. He thought maybe some tattooed, drug-crazed teenaged truants were throwing a party in one of the empty, foreclosed homes on the block. But as he moseyed along, he realized the music was coming from Fred and Lula's, and he knew a rowdy party was out of the question. About all Fred and Lula ever did for fun was drive to the casino up the hill and play the slot machines for an hour or two. Their kids had all grown up and moved out years ago; they never had anybody over.

Brady slowed down as he approached Fred and Lula's driveway. He thought for sure he would see Fred in the garage, but when he looked up the driveway in passing, he saw the garage door was wide open, no sign of Fred or his beat up Chevy truck.

Mary was weeding around the succulents in her front yard when she saw Brady. "Hey, Brady, what's up with Hentzel? Is he gettin' hard of hearin' or what?"

"Don't know, Mar. He's nowhere in sight."

"Probably went inside for somethin'."

"Yeah, probably. Maybe for some lemonade."

"Yeah, it's a scorcher for March for sure." Mary rubbed the back of her hand across her forehead.

"Uh huh, I'm panting, just like my dog."

"I've gotta go tell him to turn it down though. There's only so much of that country garbage a person can take."

"I hear you, sister." He tipped his Giants cap and shuffled off.

Mary threw the weeds in her compost bin and walked across the street. Since she was friends with Lula, she felt comfortable walking right through the garage and into the house while Lula was still at her reception job at the community credit union.

On the kitchen table Mary found a legal pad with a note scratched in Fred's sprawling hand: "Dearest Lula, I'm so sorry about last night, my love. I can only imagine what you must think of me, lying to you all these years. I hope you have it in your heart to forgive me. If so, meet me out at The Golden Cup tonight. I'll be waiting with open arms. If not, I'll just push off, and you'll never have to bother with me again. Always yours, Freddy"

Mary sat down at the table, rereading the note several times. Then she ripped it from the pad, folded it several times and put it in her pocket. Lula would be

| THE NEIGHBORLY THING

bewildered and sad at Fred's disappearance, of course, but Mary figured it would pass soon enough.

She turned off the music and closed the garage door on her way out. Back at home, she unfolded the note and put it through her shredder. Then she went to the kitchen, pulled her favorite knife from a drawer, grabbed some lemons from a bowl on the counter and started slicing. She would take some lemonade over to Lula later on. It would be the neighborly thing to do, to see that her friend was hydrated while she kept vigil through the night, waiting for her husband to walk through the door.

Long Gone

Perched on the rickety wooden rail, I look down at the hound whining and pacing along the shore. In the water, a straw hat bobs against the rocks at the river's edge. I stand tall, take a deep breath and dive from the bridge. I'm a strong swimmer. If the person who owns the hat is in distress, I figure I can help.

But the current is stronger than I'd thought, and the water far colder. I struggle to reach the surface, but each time I grab a short breath, I am pulled back under.

Finally, I grab a branch jutting into the water. I inch along the wooden limb to the shore and claw myself up onto the bank. I'm about a mile down river from the bridge. I stop to let my heart beat return to normal and then find a path running along the river and walk back to the bridge.

About half a dozen people are at the rail. They're throwing rose petals into the water. I walk to the rail and look down. The hat and hound are gone.

I ask the person closest to me, a gray-haired woman chewing on a cigar, "Did you see a hound a little while ago, pacing along the shore?" I point to where the canine had been.

"Ah, sonny, that would be ole Buddy, best darn dog there ever was," she replies.

"What do you mean 'was'? I just saw it there before I dove in. I thought maybe the owner of the hat was down in the water."

"You were right about that, 'cept you're ten years

too late, kid. My Winston was fishin' right here off the bridge, and he fell in. Don't know how it happened. Nobody saw. But Buddy must have run down to the water and gone in after him. They were found two days later way down river. Buddy's jaws were clenched tight on Winston's shirt, but they were both long gone. Today's the 10-year anniversary, sorry to say. That's why we're here on the bridge. Winston loved his rose garden. I keep it up the best I can, you know, in his memory an' all."

I reach into my pants pocket, thankful my car keys hadn't fallen into the river. I bid the woman farewell before heading to my Subaru parked at a pullout a few feet from the bridge. As I drive away, I look over my shoulder. Not one soul is on the bridge.

Drawn In

I stand still in the sweet-potato sand. It's finely ridged like a miniature zen garden raked for hours to crested perfection. I can feel Mom right behind me, despairing. I'd like to tell her to stay back, to step not a hair closer, but I can't.

I didn't expect to end up here, part of this eerie landscape, a world apart from the nearest heartbeat. I was just going to chill at Rod's house for a while after my dad burst into the house, barreled down the hall like an angry rhinoceros and knocked straight into me. I hoped the worst was over as I crumpled to the floor. So what if I'd shoplifted a pair of high tops from Target, or tried to anyway—doesn't every kid do that at one time or another?

"Get up, Joey, you sorry excuse for a son," Dad growled, fists clenched. I could barely breathe. I couldn't get up. He yanked my T-shirt. "I said, get up, you ungrateful sonofa—"

Mom ran up and pulled him away. "Brian, stop. You're like a, a ticking pizza. Didn't you ever, um, stick your foot in the compost when you were young?"

"I never embarrassed my family like this. This is a small town, Gracie. Everyone will know." He pushed her away, but not all that hard. He was calming down. "But what do you know about being embarrassed. You can't even talk right. Ticking pizza." He rolled his eyes.

"He's a good bubble overall, Brian, like a contented little piggie, you know? Why don't you go get changed. Foodies will be ready in an arc, and we can all talk."

"You're seeing him through rose-colored glasses, as always."

"I prefer my roses in glasses, dear," Mom said.

Dad shook his head. "I don't know what's going to come of us. I really don't." He stepped into the master bedroom and closed the door.

I sat up. Mom knelt down and stroked my buzz cut. "It's okay. It'll be okay. You know you'll always be the dried fig of his eye."

That was it. I'd had enough of my dad's jabs and the weird comforts of my psycho mom. I got up, yanked the keys to the Camry from the hook at the door and took off. I stopped at Rod's, but nobody was there, so I got back in the car and started driving. Before I knew it I was on 101 at the 92 exit. I headed west into the fog and followed the road to Aunt Betty's old house, even though she doesn't live there anymore.

I rode into this pencil-tip town. One of those you'll-miss-it-if-you-blink places where we always used to stop. It had been years since I'd been there. I pulled over and parked by the general store. I went inside and got a chocolate chip ice cream cone. Then I strolled along the sidewalk and saw this little art museum that Mom and I always visited while Dad read the newspaper in the car. The museum was just like I remembered it. Even the potbellied guard was the same, squinting at me, clearing his throat and telling me to keep my hands off the paintings.

I stood in front of my favorite one and lost track

of time until the guard tapped me on the shoulder and told me it was closing time. I didn't want to leave, so I spent the night in the car, and as soon as the doors opened the next day, I went inside. The painting that lured me in is a desert scene, but the colors are brighter than a real desert. The lizard is a pulsating kelly green, the cactus a neon turquoise. And the sky is swept with vibrant colors. I wanted to touch the painting, but the old guard was keeping his eyes on me from his corner stool. But then a phone rang from another room, and he dashed off.

I knew the orange sand was just acrylic on canvas, but I wanted to touch it anyway. So I reached out, and it wasn't hard like I expected. It was smooth and warm, and I filled up with this kind of light, the way people talk about spiritual experiences I've never been able to relate to, and all of a sudden, I was here inside this colorful desolation.

I can't move. I'm just here, looking at a broken down green truck next to the cactus, purple mountains in the distance, the marvelously exploding sunset sky. My mother is leaning close behind me.

"Joey, Joey is that you?" she says.

I pray that she doesn't reach out her hand. Heavy footsteps approach. "Come on, Gracie. We've got to go now. You promised you'd just be a minute," my dad says.

"Look, Brian. That's Joey in the painting. He's wearing the T-shirt and jeans he had on the day he left. He's discovered the sands of rhyme."

"Stop spouting that gibberish and come with me."

She sighs. "Oh, Brian, why can't you see?"

"Come along, Gracie."

There's a pause. Then footsteps. Then quiet.

But she'll be back. And sooner or later she'll touch my arm or leg, and she'll be drawn in too. I'll spend eternity listening to her, and that might be worse than standing here alone.

Counting

It is after he rolls off of her that the sandbag of shame lands on her chest, before she can even consider her options. He stands up, puts the knife he'd held at her throat in his back pocket and zips up his pants with fingers that look like striped Twinkies in his cheap knit gloves.

They are just like the gloves she'd seen hanging by the checkout line at the drugstore last week. She'd wondered at the time why anyone would buy them. Now she is trying to ignore the stench of the masked man who could have purchased that very pair, could have been watching her even then.

He slinks to her side, leans down and growls into her ear, tells her to count to 500 before she moves a muscle or he'll come back and finish her off. She doesn't dare even blink.

He lifts the screen he'd sliced silently while she slept what seems a lifetime ago. He slips outside to the fire escape and descends. She counts silently to 100, then 200, 300, 400, 500 and beyond to 900, 1,000, 2,000, 3,000, 5,000, 10,000, 20,000, 50,000, 100,000—on and on she counts.

Through the sunrise she counts and then through the sunset. She counts until the moon comes out and hangs so close to her window it's as though someone has swept the earth's atmosphere completely away. Her tears begin to flow, and the sand pours out. She lifts her arm, rolls over and picks up her cell phone from the headboard where she'd left it the night before.

Something Ordinary

She is Jennifer Lopez minus the talent, drive and beauty; he is Bill Gates without the intellect and wealth. They eye each other at the corner gas station and store where she gasses up her Prius before dashing inside to buy the *Press Democrat*. He fills his ancient Volvo sedan before pulling $1.10 from his pocket for the *Chronicle*. His is the better paper, he thinks. Hers is the better car, she is sure.

His heart aches when he stands behind her in the checkout line. Her thick brown hair and slender frame remind him of his daughter whose National Guard unit deployed to Iraq more than a year ago.

She hands the clerk a five dollar bill for her paper. The man behind her clears his throat. She holds out her palm to accept her change. He coughs. She turns her face toward him, raises an eyebrow. He looks like she imagines her father would if his helicopter hadn't been shot down in Vietnam when she was five years old. "You okay, man?"

"Ah, um, yeah, it's just the cold, I guess, you know, makes my throat dry or something."

She points to the cough drops on display near the cash register. "Try the Ricola; they're the best."

"Thanks," the man says. But he doesn't buy cough drops. When he returns to his Volvo, the young woman is pulling away. He smiles at her and wonders why his daughter can't be home doing something ordinary like getting gas and picking up the paper. She smiles back and wonders why he got to live and her dad had to die.

Feral Cats

She fed feral cats, which was a great nuisance to her neighbors in the Willington district, but everyone tolerated the mismatched, cracked bowls spread across her front porch and yard, the cats hissing at one another and passers by. They ignored the sight of her unruly white hair, crazed eyes and tattered trench coat as she ambled daily to the corner store for a pack of cigarettes and who knows what else she carried back in her little brown grocery sack. She was the last remaining daughter of the Willington clan, which had settled the region generations ago.

Her closest neighbor, David, an old geezer himself, helped her now and then, trimming and watering her honeysuckle hedge, mowing the lawn, washing the old Rolls Royce that sat unused in her withering garage. Word had it that she was once a real looker with a philanthropic bent, until some grifter wormed his way into her bank account, which he promptly cleaned out just before leaving town.

Most nights her neighbors could hear her singing *Some Enchanted Evening* as she stood at her kitchen sink and watered African violets long after dark, when the town's children were sound asleep in bed and the adults were turning off the TV, turning out the lights, locking the doors.

Many in Willington heard a strange noise on the last night she sang. People described it in different ways. Was it a scream? A laugh? An exclamation of joy? It depends on who's talking. Then came another

| FERAL CATS

sustained sound from within her rundown home. Some say it was a vacuum cleaner; others say it was something more sinister, like a chainsaw, muffled somehow. All agree that it droned on and on.

After that night nobody saw her or her Rolls Royce again. David tended the hedge and lawn until some distant relative of hers had the old house torn down. The lot was sold, a new showcase home built that sold for over $1.5 million the first time. But there is a problem with the cats. They writhe around on the lawn and meow like they own the place. Each new owner enlists the help of animal control officers to have the cats caught and shipped to a shelter. But every time it happens, even more cats come to replace them.

The new house is empty now, neglected; the list price is $225,000. There are no takers. And every so often when lights are being turned out around the neighborhood, and people are yawning as they prepare for bed, someone hears what sounds like a woman singing *Some Enchanted Evening* right where the old woman's kitchen window used to be.

Four Blocks Away

Sam and Sharon hustle down the boulevard in their electric car. He is driving, tapping his fingers on the wheel to the beat of Lady Gaga's *Born This Way* playing on the oldies station. Sharon looks out the window at the median, its palms, poppies and daisies meticulously maintained. This she appreciates.

They stop at a red light. Sharon is soothed by this routine switch from green to yellow to red, even though there is no need for traffic control. Rarely do more than four cars zoom along the boulevard at any given time. She is bolstered by the lore about the elders, who put aside their differences, dismissed their PR firms and lobbyists and figured out how to maintain a semblance of normalcy back in 2020, when people were rioting throughout the world because no human baby had been born alive since 2015.

That was almost three decades ago. She and Sam were among the last born. They speed past sparkling high rises, once bustling with life, now empty, but still washed, lit up and manicured for a future everyone hopes will come. The hospital is four blocks away. Sharon's pains are three minutes apart. The obstetrician waits, gown, gloves and mask on. Sharon bows her head in prayer.

I'll Have to Tell Him

My Bernie's a real good man, except he gets these harebrained ideas. I try my darnedest to put the kibosh on them—like befriending Jake the Wolfman. We called him that 'cause he kept wolves, well, not really wolves, but wolf dogs, half wolf, half dog, which some folks say are worse than wolves because they have instincts pointing them every which way.

I didn't take to the idea of the Wolfman, but my Bernie's the most curious guy in all of North Bend, and the friendliest, too. He's a mail carrier and he got this route a few years back that included Jake the Wolfman's spread. They started by sayin' hi, and then a few friendly words, you know, how's the wife doin' or those sure are pretty critters you have there. Pretty soon Bernie was savin' Jake the Wolfman's mail 'til last and then shootin' the breeze on his front porch for an hour or so before comin' home, which I didn't appreciate, and I told Bernie so.

But, you know, I couldn't stay mad about it because Bernie has this sheepish grin that gets to me, so he can get away with anything, darn it. And after a while I guess I started to look forward to his stories about what was new with Jake the Wolfman because, let's face it, things are pretty boring here in North Bend—just lots of us sittin' around with nothin' to do and nothin' but dreams left of jobs that went south of the border or to Asia or wherever.

So Jake the Wolfman had about a dozen of 'em in a big enclosure, about four acres. And he went in there and ran around with them, said the wolf dogs were his brothers. He tried to get Bernie to go in with him. Bernie swears he never did because a dozen of them crazy wolf dogs was just too much for him. But he did say one-on-one those wolf dogs were as sweet as can be and a little mysterious, too, like something out of a myth. I told him right then and there that was a big bunch of hooey. Oh, but Bernie looked so stricken by my words, I wished I could have taken 'em back.

Then Bernie came home one day real down in the dumps. He flopped on his recliner and sat starin' at the TV, which wasn't even on, mind you. And I said Bernie, what in the dickens has gotten into you, and he grunted a little but couldn't get a word out for a long time, but I kept askin', and finally he said those wolf dogs had up and killed Jake the Wolfman.

Bernie said when he pulled up in the mail van, an ambulance was driving away, and police and animal control officers and even North Bend's fire captain were swarming around the property. Dead wolf dogs were stacked in a pile just inside the enclosure, and Bernie saw a pool of blood at the gate. There were a lot of tears that night between the two of us, I'll tell you. Bernie was sobbing, and I was cryin' for Bernie, and then I was wailin' for Jake the Wolfman, even though I didn't even know him. And I was cryin' about maybe having to let go of a fantasy Bernie had, and I was starting to have, too, about things being different than they really are between people and wild animals.

| I'LL HAVE TO TELL HIM

We were still weepy the next morning when Bernie went off to work. I expected we'd be glum at the end of the day, too. But Bernie returned at suppertime with that sheepish grin of his and a big bulge in his jacket. I asked, what's in there, but he kept mum. He sat in his chair, unzipped the jacket, and there were two little pups, couldn't have been more than eight weeks old. He'd gone to Jake the Wolfman's house, sat on the front porch to just think about his pal, and he heard squealing coming from the direction of the enclosure. He went inside and found the pups huddled way back in a corner behind a pile of bricks.

Bernie asked me if he could keep them. He looked so hopeful, and the pups looked so cute snuggled there in the chair, I said okay. I said it real stern, like a cop, so as not to let on how adorable I thought the little critters were. I insisted these half-wild animals live out back in the yard, though, for our own peace of mind. Bernie said he was okay with that.

We built a dog house out back and told the neighbors our pups are sled-dog mutts, so everything is cool with them. Each day Bernie feeds them their breakfast kibble before he goes off to work. When he leaves, I wave goodbye from the front door. Then I bring the babies inside. I never expected to turn into a wolf-person. But when I look into their blue eyes, I know they understand me in ways not even Bernie does. My Bernie. Pretty soon I'll have to tell him about the pups and me because, well, two of them babies just isn't enough.

What For

Pierce wakes up the morning after. Yolanda, still sleeping beside him, had been wrong about the world coming to an end. He wonders how his wife of twelve years, the mother of his children, could have been so stupid, so snookered in. Yolanda had even seemed disappointed last night when they'd watched the news on TV. Not much had happened: a twister ravaged a section of southern Nebraska; another levee broke along the Mississippi; a plane carrying 186 people disappeared over New Hampshire; a 5.5 earthquake hit San Luis Obispo, California; a few terrorists were detained at O'Hare airport and managed to shoot a customs agent before they were overpowered. But that was it.

Pierce smiles at the sunshine coming through the bedroom curtains, as it always does on clear days. He swings his legs to the side of the bed and slides his feet into his comfy, fleece slippers. He takes a step, but there is no floor beneath him. He falls down, down into a vast, black sky, and spins far away from his home, his neighborhood, his life.

He screams as he loses sight of the earth, and Yolanda stirs in her dream. She wakes up and wonders where Pierce is. It isn't like him to leave for work without kissing her goodbye.

She sits up and stretches while swinging her legs to the side of the bed. She slides her feet into her slippers and stands up. The floorboards creak as she makes her way down the hall and looks in on her children, still asleep, surrounded by stuffed animals in their beds. She smiles and shuffles into the kitchen, where she sees that Pierce didn't take out the garbage last night; of course, she thinks, he was too busy hounding her about what a fool she was for believing the world was about to end. Irked, she pulls the garbage bag up from the can and vows she'll give Pierce what for when he comes home.

Life Along the Coast

He sees her perched, like a romance novel heroine, at the precipice. A fringe of permed curls dances around her oval face; the skirt of her shirtwaist dress slaps at her shins. She is on the wrong side of the guard rail, clinging to it with both hands as she leans backward toward the ocean.

Other people are closer to her, but they don't seem to see her. He runs across the parking lot toward the lookout point. He waves his arms and calls, "Stop her. She's about to jump. Look!"

She lets one hand go of the rail. He runs faster. She loses her footing and slips, one hand barely hanging on. He closes in. She loses her grip. He leaps. But he misses his mark and tumbles over the edge of the continent. He plummets, bouncing against jagged boulders until his body hits the beach far below.

Later, witnesses say it happened so fast, they hadn't really had time to react. The man had pulled into the parking lot, gotten out of his car, run to the cliff and gone over. He hadn't even closed his car door. He'd screamed something on his way, but nobody could make out what it was.

The sheriff wonders why at least one young man runs to his death like that every summer and why a pair of peep-toe platform heels is often found near the body. All he can figure is the lookout must be some kind of draw for guys who have no hope and for gals who like to throw shoes. He chalks it up as just another part of life along the coast.

The Wrong Man

Myrna sits on the steps of an abandoned library building. Crime fighters amble in and out of the police station across the street. With badges and guns worn proudly, they laugh, slap each other on the back, sip coffee. Myrna stares. Down the street, her twins tumble the morning away in preschool.

It's been four weeks since her husband, Edward Blayne, was killed at their front door. She and the twins were at the park when it happened. She remembers the glow of the sun on her children's skin as she pushed them in the swings, the perfection of their little feet pattering through the sand after they jumped out and wiggled to the wading pool. Then later, all the blood at their threshold and Edward in an ambulance unconscious, and the muscled arms that held her back, the voices that said she could not ride with him. And her babies crying.

The officers who shot him swear Edward brandished a gun when he opened the door. They say he cocked it and refused to put it down. Myrna knows he had no gun. An Iraq War vet, Edward was through with war, through with violence of any kind.

A lawyer sympathetic to Myrna's cause says the officers paid a visit to the wrong man; they meant to raid Eddie Blaine, a drug kingpin who lives on the other side of town. In a few minutes, the lawyer will meet Myrna on the steps. They will cross the street together, and Myrna will ask, once again, when her husband's body will be released.

Never, Ever

Seventeen-year-old Georgie had a drinking problem. He'd had so many beers at so many parties in the last several years that he was notorious throughout the county for it. But he begged his parents to let him drive their refurbished 1944 John Deere in the Fourth of July parade. His folks agreed on the condition that he not drink a drop of beer. They were pleased with the plan because it meant they could drive their 1959 Chevy Impala in the parade, which would automatically enter it into the classic car competition.

After all the red-white-and-blue bedecked floats, children on horseback, shining vehicles, clowns, bubble machines and the odd chicken or two had moseyed down Main Street, and the smell of barbeque chicken permeated the noontime air, Georgie bid farewell to his folks and headed home. They stayed behind to visit friends they rarely saw because their ranch was up on the mountain far from town, and the road to their property was one lane, winding and treacherous.

Georgie was feeling fine; he'd kept his word, hadn't had one drop of alcohol in any form. But seventeen-year-old Georgie had a mean streak, and it didn't take much to set him off. And on that Fourth of July, Georgie pulled up to his favorite rock formation right at the split in the road where the last leg of his journey home began. The rocks provided a panoramic view of the town, the valley that contained it and the river that led to the ocean shore in the distance.

When Georgie turned off the tractor and hopped

down, he saw a red-tailed hawk perched in his favorite spot. From his satchel, he pulled a canteen of Gatorade, a ham and cheese sandwich and wasp spray. Then he crept up the rock and blasted the hawk with the spray. The hawk flew up into a nearby oak. Georgie took over his favorite spot and began his picnic. Unaware the hawk was growing inch by inch in the branches behind him, he chewed and enjoyed the view.

When Georgie returned to his tractor some of the oak's branches were almost touching the ground under the now coyote-size hawk's weight, but Georgie didn't notice. He started up the tractor, turned off the highway and began chugging up the hill toward home. The hawk pursued, growing larger with each flap of its wings and casting a shadow over him. He assumed a cloud was passing overhead until the hawk descended and he saw the immense claws grab the tractor.

Up, up, up the hawk flew until it hovered over the highest point of the ridge. Then it let go. The tractor broke apart as it tumbled down the side of the mountain into a gorge. Georgie fell into a pine, which kept him from plunging to his death.

When he awoke in the hospital, his parents were at his bedside. He'd only broken a couple of ribs and a leg. They were furious about the tractor but pleased to inform him that their Impala had won the classic car competition. They didn't believe his story about the hawk. The John Deere is rusting in the gorge. And his folks say Georgie will never, ever drive their Impala.

Disappointed

Jeffrey's hands grip the slender ledge at the bottom of the overpass; his feet dangle above a freeway ominously empty at 8 a.m.

"I know it hurts, son, but you've gotta hold on," says an old man in a 49ers cap who had called 911 and brought the morning commute to a standstill. "Hold on, and it'll get better. I swear."

The old man stretches down over the rail, but his hands are about a foot shy of Jeffrey's wrists. Jeffrey grunts. His arms ache. His fingers and ears itch. Tears roll down his face. He didn't think letting go would be like trying to peel his skin off. It was supposed to have been over long before the sunrise, the TV news coverage, the traffic jams.

A helicopter hovers overhead as a negotiator strides up and orders the old man to step away. The old man straightens up, steps back. The negotiator clears his throat. Jeffrey loosens his grip, looking up at the helicopter's blades slicing the clear blue sky as he falls backward, unaware that a net stretches below him just in time to break his fall, just in time to force him into another day.

The old man rips off his cap, pulls a pen from his front pocket, scratches his phone number on the bill. He lunges back to the rail and tosses the cap over the edge. It floats down and lands on Jeffrey's stomach as he bounces, disappointed, in the net.

How Dreadful

Wending her way toward Harold's Diner at the end of the block, Gloria pauses to touch one of the many red roses blooming along the picket fence defining Judy's front yard. Judy scowls from her parlor window as she knits a hat for a baby yet to be conceived. Judy's husband works long hours in a cubicle, balancing accounts for his employer. Gloria's husband left her for a pole dancer a year ago.

Gloria spies Judy peeking from behind her curtains. She continues on her way, feeling sorry for the woman inside who never shares recipes with neighbors or stops in for a cup of coffee at Harold's. At the corner, she opens the diner door and is greeted by familiar smells and the smiles of long-time friends.

The diner door closes behind Gloria. Judy frowns, imagining how dreadful being a waitress must be.

A Dove Coos

With the shadows of maple leaves dancing across her face, she rests in a hammock that has seen better days. He pours lemonade and offers it to her, ice clinking against glass. She lifts her hand up but snaps it under the comforter when she sees her mottled fingers tremble.

He puts the glass on the wrought iron table by her side. A dove coos nearby. He bends down, tucks a stray strand of white hair behind her ear and wraps the comforter tighter around her slender frame. She closes her eyes.

He stifles a sob, unable to envision a world that lacks her head on the pillow next to his, her dark blue eyes a lighthouse guiding his way.

I Don't Suppose

The coleus on the counter caught my eye. It was in my kitchen, but I'd never seen it before, and it looked ghastly with my blue and yellow decor. I called my long-time neighbor Layna and told her a stranger was in my home and she'd better come over quick and save me. She asked, "How do you know there's a stranger there?" I said, "Because there's a coleus on my counter, and I know it didn't walk in by itself."

She told me she'd seen the plant just yesterday when she'd come over to borrow my Shark mop. I told her she was mistaken and that it was three days ago she borrowed the mop anyway, not yesterday. She told me I was full of you know what. And we went on arguing like that until I said, "You bring back my Shark right now or I'm gonna throw this damn plant at your picture window."

Now I'm sitting on my front porch steps, plant in my lap. She's standing on her porch, Shark in hand. I was all set to march across the road and let her have it, but I just noticed there's this pink, plastic rabbit stuck smack in the middle of my rosebush hedge, and I swear I've never seen that critter before. What if this is the beginning of my end, what if I'm slipping terrified into that good night? Layna's my best friend. I don't suppose I ought to brain her.

Better Things to Do

He pads to his office window and opens the blinds. Sun bathing his face, he loosens his shirt collar, sighs, closes his eyes. The warmth lulls him, and he groans, repelled at the thought of the presentation slides in his laptop. He gulps a breath and another and another as sunbeams flow in and around and through him, filling every crevice in the room. Then his phone beeps, a reminder of the morning staff meeting.

He spins from the window, snatches his laptop and dashes out his office door. His mind crackles with percentages and profit margins as he darts toward the conference room. Racing through the reception area, he glances in the wall mirror and sees a halo pulsating around his head. A 21st century Jesus, he has a halo, a halo.

He drops his laptop on the reception desk, rips off his employee badge and slaps that on the desk, too. Then he struts out the front door. His father is calling him. He has better things to do than stay at work.

She'll Be Ready

She runs down the sidewalk in the dark, block after block, until she reaches the end, the dead end, fenced off. She squints at the wide-open field beyond, the goats under an oak, an old tractor rusted. Heart pounding, she climbs up the fence, jumps over the barbed wire top and hides behind the tractor.

Minutes later, he arrives, rifle in hand. She trembles as shots ricochet off her metal refuge. She trembles as lights turn on all along the street, as a distant police siren grows louder, closer. She trembles when he is cuffed and pushed, swearing, into the police van. And she trembles as she packs a bag and calls a cab for the airport.

Thousands of miles away now, she pumps iron, runs marathons, teaches karate. If he finds her, she'll be ready.

Squished a Spider

While sipping her morning coffee, Clara noticed a big, black spider ambling across the rug near her feet. She stood up, ready to stomp the thing, but then she sneezed several times. When she opened her eyes, she spied the creature scurrying away. Rather than whack it before it found cover, Clara took the sneezes as a sign and let the spider be. Soon, she forgot about the spider lurking in her home.

That night in her dreams spiders covered the walls of her bedroom; they crawled in and out of her mouth and ears; they perched on everything she owned. She screamed and cursed and tried to bat them off, but the spiders didn't budge. She fought on anyway for what seemed like eons until, completely spent, she dropped her flailing arms and said, "Go ahead then. Kill me. Take me. Do what you will." At that, the spiders vanished and the dream shifted into placid territory.

The next day, as she watered a fuchsia hanging in her garden outside, Clara took a step backward and inadvertently squished a spider. She didn't notice the dead arachnid underfoot, and she never dreamed of spiders again.

She Couldn't Wait

He lost his soul on the Sundial Bridge up in Redding. That girl Ava did it. She sashayed across, her camisole straps sliding down her bare shoulders, her Coach sunglasses shielding her gaze from sunlight reflecting off the Sacramento River.

She smiled. He smiled back. She paused, said hi. He stopped too, said hello and imagined sitting across from her at a dimly lit bistro, their knees touching beneath a wobbly table. She slid her sunglasses to the top of her head. He looked into her eyes and saw ebony ovals, no irises, pupils or whites. Just solid black nothingness sucking him into a deep, endless, terrifying space.

He fell, screaming to the bridge's glass and granite deck. She bent over, laughed into his ear, stole his wallet and called 911. She told the dispatcher her name was Ava; she was just another tourist enjoying the bridge when a young man suddenly collapsed in mid span; he must have hit his head; he wasn't moving. She said she couldn't wait for the EMTs; she had to catch the charter to Yosemite Falls.

Late that night at the hospital, he rose from his bed and walked to the bathroom. He turned on the light, looked into the mirror and saw his eyes were crow-black just like hers. He slipped out of the hospital unnoticed, swiping a pair of Prada sunglasses from an unattended nurse's station along the way. Now he traverses the country, searching for Ava, one landmark to the next.

Drifting

She is a rainbow fading as she loads the laundry. He is an old Chevy idling on the couch. He sees a brilliant arch of color turning as she reaches for the Tide. She turns toward him and sees a fast ride down a dirt road on a long-ago sun-burned evening.

She shakes the detergent box and hears seashell and driftwood chimes. She pours the powder into the washer, closes the lid, turns the dial. The machine rumbles, the waterfall comes.

"What would you like for lunch?" she asks.

The coffee table is a creaking pier, the carpet a beach of turquoise sand. "I think I'd like ..."

He closes his eyes and becomes a boat drifting in a leather sea. She sits in the rocker facing him. She rocks. She rocks. She rocks and becomes the wind. She becomes the wind blowing him to shore.

He opens his eyes.

"What would you like for lunch?" she asks.

My First Love

I know what he did. I live in a forest, not a cave. It's just that when he came to my door, fear dripping off him like sweat, eyes wild as oil over flames, I saw the boy he used to be, the one who gave me my first corsage, the one who took me over the moon and back.

A SWAT team has the woods surrounded. They're looking for a cold-blooded killer. When they knocked at my door I told them I haven't seen him even though he's in my pump house just a dozen feet away.

Bullets ricochet in the canyon below my cabin. I don't know what those lawmen are shooting at. Their prey is already bound and gagged. See, he wooed me and dumped me long ago. I'm going to get my due after dark before anyone else lays a hand on him. Does this make me a bad person? I guess so. But he was my first love.

Snow Colors

Ready for bed, Little Toby looks out his window and sees glowing snowflakes of red, green, gold and white falling through the dark sky. He wants to tell his mom and dad about the colors in the snow, but they are arguing in the next room, and they always get angry with him if he interrupts when one or the other of them is pacing or throwing dishes or pounding the wall or threatening divorce. So he tiptoes through the house, past the Christmas tree in the living room and to the hallway where he puts on his boots and slips out the front door.

Toby prances around the yard, his face up and arms out to welcome the twinkling flakes as they land on his skin and pajamas. His parents' voices fade into the background. He begins to spin like a dervish and hum *Joy to the World*. He spins across the yard, across the sidewalk and into the street just as a Toyota rounds the corner.

The driver sees the boy, brakes, swerves and comes to a halt in the driveway of Toby's home. The driver, who is a neighbor dressed in a Santa suit after a shift posing for pictures with tots at Macy's, gets out of the car and runs into the street to pick up Toby, who is still spinning and entranced by the snowflakes.

"Santa, where's your sleigh?" Toby asks as Santa carries him to his front door.

"In the shop getting serviced for the big journey tomorrow." Santa puts him down.

"Did you bring me the colored snow?"

| SNOW COLORS

Santa studies the snow and sees that it is, indeed, multicolored. "Well, I'll be. It is in full color, isn't it."

Toby opens the door and steps inside. His parents are still arguing.

"Can you do something about them?" Toby asks.

"I'm afraid I'm better with toys, you know."

"Thanks for the snow then," Toby says.

"Sure, kid." Santa waves and walks back to his car.

Toby takes off his boots and returns to his room as Santa backs his Toyota out of the driveway. Toby's parents are now quiet; the falling snow is white. He pulls out *Where The Wild Things Are* from under his bed, gets under the covers and waits for one of them to tuck him in.

Since the Accident

Since the accident, the sun shines only at half mast and wrens roost in other yards. All day, she looks out the window as pine needles fall to the ground. At night, he drinks alone in the den while she knits in the bedroom.

Since the accident, soot falls from the clouds and rats nibble on the insulation in their attic. Over breakfast, wishful thinking dilutes memories of that day, so that no gouge remains in the trunk of an old oak tree; their Camry is not scorched; a blue tricycle is no longer smashed at the side of the road; a child is not struggling for each breath in a hospital bed.

He opens the front door and steps onto a porch stabbed with icicles. He walks down the empty driveway and into the street. She follows. Hand in hand they amble down blocks they used to know but no longer recognize. Horns blare for them to get out of the road. They pause at a curb, each one wanting to go home, neither one knowing the way.

Tears Will Slow

I knew right away I had to have her. I should have expected she'd fight me like a badger. She held her boy's head high as my waves tore at her flesh. She held on longer than I ever thought possible, pulling strength from something beyond my depths.

At last, a surfer's hands grabbed the boy, steadied him on a board. But when the hands reached for her, I, Poseidon, snatched her and pulled her home to me.

She, like her family above, is despairing now. But their tears will slow eventually. Her husband will remarry; her son will grow up; her friends will stop talking about her. And then, she will turn her fierce blue eyes toward me. She will be mine forever.

Thanks, I Guess

I want to throw one of those huge Oxford-type dictionaries at him, iron his ears flat to his skull, shrink him to toy poodle size and throw him so hard against the patio door that the glass breaks and he tumbles bloody and broken to the slab outside.

Jeez! Did I really just say that? Man, I'm messed up.

The doorbell is ringing; I'm sure it's for him. His half-eaten pizza has grown hard and cold on a TV tray, as usual. His papers are strewn all over his bedroom floor. His dirty underwear is balled up by the toilet. I could go on and on. Living with a 13-year-old boy sure isn't easy.

Of course he can't bother to get up and answer the door. So it's up to me to get it just like it's up to me to do everything else around here. That's what a mom does, after all.

Damn, hold your horses, door person, whoever you are. I'm coming, already. People don't have an ounce of patience anymore. What? You're here to deliver a package? Well, gosh thanks, I guess. So what are you standing ... Oh, You want a tip? Sure, yeah, everybody wants something these days. Hold on a sec. I've got a couple dollars in my purse right here. ... There you go.

Well, let's see here. Man, this lid is tough, but I think I can pry it off. There now. What is that? A head? Somebody's head? Oh, no, no, no. This isn't happening. No, no, no, no. This looks like ... What the?

Get in here right this minute, Sonny. Right now or

| THANKS, I GUESS

I'm going to slap you to kingdom come. Right now, you mental case. Right this minute.

So, is this what I think it is? ... But why did you kill him and why the fuck did you send me his head? ... Oh, for Christ's sake. I never meant all that shit I said about him. He was your father. Your father! ... I can't believe it. You thought it would make me happy? ... Oh, you're sorry, are you? Get out of my sight, you moron. Go to your room. Go, go, go. I need some time to think.

This is bad, really bad. The head I can just dump in the river, or something. But who's going to take him off my hands on Wednesday nights and every other weekend now? Jeez. I'll probably have to pay somebody to keep any eye on him, the little fucker.

When She Wakes Up

My niece Emma's a little different. It started after a family rafting trip turned tragic when she was twelve. Her mom, dad and brother all drowned when the raft overturned. Emma was found downstream hours later, badly bruised but alive.

When she came to live with me right after that, all Emma could talk about was how one of those Bigfoot creatures had plunged into the rapids and saved her. I did my best to bring her down gently to the reality that it's fun to tell stories about Bigfoot sightings around campfires, but only crackpots believe they actually exist.

Emma never did accept my point of view on that, though, or on much of anything else either. And when she finished high school she went to live in the woods way up north in Humboldt County instead of going to college. Like I said, she's a little different.

Last week she called and asked if she could come for a visit. I said yes, of course. Then she said she'd just had a baby girl with her boyfriend and she was bringing the baby, too. She said her boyfriend wasn't coming though because he hates to travel. Well, I didn't even know she had a boyfriend, let alone a baby. But that doesn't matter. I was thrilled to see her and the baby when they arrived this morning. The tyke was all wrapped up and sleeping, though. Emma was tired, too, so they went to take a nap in Emma's old room.

Before she fell asleep Emma told me that if the baby cried, to just leave her alone—no matter what.

But a little while ago, the little one started sobbing, and it tore at my heart. I decided to tend to her. That way Emma could keep on sleeping.

I tiptoed into the room and picked up the babe. She was wiggling and wailing so hard I thought, what harm could it do to loosen the blanket a bit and uncover the baby's face so she could get some air? But as soon as I lifted the blanket flap, I felt no more weight in my arms. I saw no face, no body. The blanket held only silence, stillness.

I put the blanket down by Emma right where it had been and ran out of the room. My heart is still racing at the sight. I know I heard that baby crying, felt her squirm in my arms. Now, Emma's odd. I've always accepted that. But this goes way beyond anything I could have imagined. What on earth am I going to do when she wakes up?

Music for Ghosts

Sleepless and in pain, Mireille hears murmuring by her bedroom window. She looks out and sees familiar translucent forms gathering in the darkness along the backyard fence. She angles into the wheelchair at the side of the bed, lifts a mandolin from her cluttered dressing table, and maneuvers out of the bedroom through the house and down the ramp into her yard.

There she sees them, swaying like silver leaves in the breeze: her mother and father, husband, grandparents, sister, brothers, best friends from childhood, the son who died while a babe in the crib—all her loved ones lost from the many stages of her long life.

She picks up the mandolin and begins to pluck as though arthritis had never invaded her fingers. Her loved ones surround her and dance—she strong as the maypole, they light as ribbons. She plays on until, hours later, she closes her eyes and drops the mandolin into her lap.

Mireille's daughter stops by later and finds her mother in the yard, sleeping to the rising sun. As daughter pushes mother back into the house and then makes hot tea, Mireille promises to stop playing music for ghosts every night. She promises to take her sleeping pills and her pain medication. She promises to play bingo at the church twice a week and attend the water aerobics class at the Y. She promises many things to get her daughter out of her hair and off to work. Then Mireille sleeps the day away in her chair, hands at peace on the mandolin resting in her lap.

Tide Pool Dreams

He eats ocean wind for breakfast; she starves on sand. Clad in love-repellant jackets, they drag race across the past. He takes the lead, then she, then he, again, back and forth all afternoon.

"Will it always be like this?" he asks at sunset.

She shrugs and slips into a tide pool dream. He follows, the unknown nipping in their wake.

The Ice Cream Vendor's Song

The day his father drove away, Danube watched the Jeep sweep the house, yard and block of laughter as it roared out of the parking place, down the street and around the corner. Danube stayed on the porch as blackbirds preened in the branches above. He remained as neighborhood friends chased the ice cream vendor's melody. He stayed on as the sun flung purples and oranges and reds across a gray-blue sky and as crickets sang into the void where his hope had been.

The first few nights after his father drove away, Danube fell asleep outside, and his mom carried him to bed. Then she insisted he come inside for supper, then earlier and earlier, for he had homework to do and chores and a future to build from marathons, tests and kisses year by year.

Now, a father himself, Danube drives a Jeep; he doesn't know why. And when he visits his mom, he sits on the front porch in the late afternoons, his arm around his son's shoulders, and he feels melancholy squeeze his heart momentarily, until he takes his child's hand and runs block to block, chasing the ice cream vendor's song.

Acknowledgements

Thank you to my husband, Jim; daughter, Moira; stepsons, Ryan and Jackson; sisters Kathy and Mary Ruth; and my uncle John. Their love, laughter and steadfast support through the years have been irreplaceable. Kathy also created this book's masterful design, both the cover and the interior.

Much appreciation to my writing partner, Claire Blotter, whose poetry and insights about the writing life always inspire me. A big shout out to my editors for this project: Dan Watkins, whose astute comments helped add new dimensions to this collection, and Ana Manwaring, whose keen eye helped polish this manuscript for prime time.

And major props to a Sonoma County treasure, Redwood Writers. The friendships, encouragement and tips shared with members of that club are gifts I wish every writer could have. And many thanks to the readers to whom I dedicate this collection.

About the Author

Laura McHale Holland is an author and indie publisher. Her childhood memoir, *Reversible Skirt*—which illustrates the far-reaching effects a parent's suicide can have on surviving children and other family members—won a silver medal in the 2011 Readers Favorite book awards.

Laura's stories and articles have appeared in such publications as *Every Day Fiction Three*, *Wisdom Has a Voice*, the *Vintage Voices* anthologies, *NorthBay biz* magazine, the *Noe Valley Voice* and the original *San Francisco Examiner*. *The Ice Cream Vendor's Song* is her first collection of flash fiction.

To keep up with her, please visit her website at: http://lauramchaleholland.com.

Also by Laura McHale Holland
Reversible Skirt, a Memoir

What people are saying about the book:

Reversible Skirt *is a thoroughly heartrending read. In her moving new memoir, author Laura McHale Holland takes the reader through the deepest recesses of grief, sorrow, and abuse – all from the fragile perspective of an innocent, unsuspecting child. What ultimately proves most impressive about Holland's spiritual sojourn is that – despite the unchecked chaos of her upbringing – she perseveres through it all with an unbreakable, sweet spirit. Such unflappable strength is highly commendable – not to mention rare – and your appreciation of Holland's genuine loving warmth is sure to grow by leaps and bounds with the turning of each fresh page. A highly recommended tale of learning to overcome the worst that life has to offer.*

– Karynda Lewis, Apex Reviews

Expertly written, a poignant and honest story of Laura, a young girl who manages to keep afloat in a world flooded with loss and abuse. Surrounded by lies and deceit, Laura's underlying strength acts like a lighthouse guiding her through a tumultuous childhood. Interspersed with sweet events that captivate and give us hope. A reminder of the resiliency of the human spirit.

– Ann E. Philipp, mystery and humor writer

Reversible Skirt *describes a time in our not-too-distant past where mental illness and suicide were swept under the rug. While we have made some gains as a society, the situation will feel familiar to those of us who have lived through mental illness in our own families. What was most intriguing about the book was how the author and her sisters forgave their abusive stepmother after everything she did to them as children. Their*

ability to survive and recover from their challenging childhoods is uplifting. The capacity they show for forgiveness is truly inspiration.
  – Michelle and Denise Nicolson, founders of Families of the Mentally Ill website

Reversible Skirt *is the tender telling of a girl's odyssey through an abusive childhood. The voice is honest. I feel as if I've known her all my life.*
  – H.B. Reid, author of The Connected *and* Nikita Khrushchev Waved to Me

Culturally surviving a family member's suicide, let alone talking of it, was just not done 50 years ago. Secrets hidden behind facades of normalcy lay the foundation of potential life long trauma. Laura McHale Holland speaks to us of such a time. A time when she and her two sisters who had yet to reach the age of five must eventually not only face the realization of their mother's self-inflicted death, but also deal with the passing of their father seven years afterward, and living with his second wife who makes Cinderlla's stepmother look like a saint. Three small girls in an affluent Chicago suburb defy the odds and come to grips with who they are and the bond they must form to survive. The story is told through Laura's young eyes beginning at three years old continuing through her early adolescence. Get ready for a full day or night of reading for once your start you will find it hard to put this book down. The sequel cannot be far behind.
  – W.T. Bonine Jr., Amazon reader

Reversible Skirt is available at Barnesandnoble.com, Amazon.com, Smashwords.com, Powells.com, and by order at local bookstores.

Lightning Source UK Ltd.
Milton Keynes UK
UKHW012029290319
340177UK00001B/93/P